The Facts of Life
(as taught by a nine year old)

Written and Illustrated by
Steffan Basdeo

CONTENTS

Based on a true story

Chapter 1

Silently, he gazed from his bedroom window. Nine-year-old T admired the starlight raves in the cloudless night sky, which he often did whenever he could. In three days, he would be turning 10 – the big double-digit age. He was growing up as all little boys did, and that meant he'd have to do away with childish ways. At least, that was what he thought.

From reading his book about stars and space multiple times, he could easily identify the planets - Venus and Mars. Even star constellations such as the Big Dipper and Orion's Belt he recognised with ease, as if they were drawn with markers in the sky. His bedroom window faced the front of the yard and his dog, Box, took notice of him.

Wagging his tail, Box walked towards T's window and sat down, looking up at him.

"I wonder, Box, when the stars in the sky turned ten, if they had to change as well," T asked his dog who responded with an 'arf'. He stared at a peculiar star he never noticed before but gave it no second thought.

"Maybe, they're not ten years old yet and share the same birthday as me," he said wondering what would have happened if it were really true. But he knew the stars in the sky were billions of years old, all from reading his book about stars and space. He began to feel sleepy, his yawns getting more frequent by the minute.

"I think I'll go to bed now," he told Box yawning some more. "See you in the morning." Box responded with an 'arf' once more and went to his cozy kennel to drift off to sleep as well. As they both slept, the peculiar star in the sky grew brighter and strayed to the left.

Chapter 2

It was Friday when T awoke the next morning, and the weather was stormy as the rain fell hard against the leaky roof of his home. Each time the lightning flashed, the thunder roared after, and it was so bright that T was able to see it through his thick bedroom curtains.

Making his way downstairs to the kitchen, Box greeted him wagging his tail furiously and licking T's foot, tickling him. His older sister, who was watching over him while their parents were away, had told him that school was cancelled due to the weather and he celebrated with a fist pump, although she still had to go to work. Another fist pump! T loved being home alone since he thought he was old enough to do so without having someone to babysit him.

"So… toast or cereal?" his sister asked him and inside his head, he was sent into a frenzy!

Fact of Life #1: Toast and Cereal are the best things on Earth

The internal battle began. He hated making the choice every morning between the best foods ever. And there was no combining the two into one super-food. Two years ago, he attempted to create the super-food: the warm, buttery goodness of toast with the sweet crunchy bliss of cereal (and milk). What became of that, he forced his taste buds to forget.

So, T created a system – one day he would have toast, and the next day he would have cereal, and the day after he would have toast again, and so on. Today was cereal day but the cold weather persuaded him to get toast instead. But if he had toast today, that meant he'd have to have cereal two days in a row afterwards, and he couldn't bear to not have toast for so long. He felt the same way towards cereal today as well. His system worked well so far, but his cravings were about to crash it.

"Toast, please," he replied with a looming thundercloud over his head (separate from the ones outside). He suddenly felt as if he placed a bad omen upon himself.

Chapter 3

The morning progressed and T was home alone watching TV in the living room with Box, who was sitting on the ground with him as the storm continued. As thunder roared loudly nonstop, he grew bored of what the TV had to offer and decided to build a fort, using cushions. He made-believe it was his own home, as if he were grown up – but maintained it was only pretend. With his birthday in two days, he did not want to do away with childish ways yet.

Suddenly, a loud crash came from the garage! Frightened, T stayed with Box in his just-completed fort, and listened carefully for any more sounds. The thunder roared once more making T jump so quickly he bumped hard onto the 'walls' causing the fort to collapse. He jolted up onto his feet, remaining alert as he stared into the direction of the garage.

Fact of Life #2: One person is all you need to be on your side

With Box at his side, T had the courage to take the first step to investigate the noise coming from the garage. He picked up a newspaper and rolled it up in his right hand, raising it into the air ready for anything. Approaching the door leading into the garage from the house, he paused in his tracks and stared at the knob. He strained his ears as hard as he could to hear any signs of breathing or a beating heart coming from the other side, but heard his own deep breathing instead.

T looked down at Box who was sniffing the crack under the door and decided it was time to be the hero. Grabbing hold of the doorknob, T held his breath and in one sudden movement he opened the door and jumped in, shouting and swinging the rolled up newspaper in front of him. Box looked around and continued sniffing around the garage filled with old boxes storing old things, and poorly lit from the heavy, overcast sky. Then, another crash came from the shelving behind him and T spun around to see paint cans topple off the shelf.

Out from the darker shadows, a wooden crate rose in the air scaring the heebie jeebies out of T! Screaming, he bolted through the doorway with Box following close behind, and slammed the door shut, locking it. Hyperventilating, he backed away as thumps, bangs, and crashes came from the dark garage. T's wild imagination showed him a monster terrorising the contents of the room and it made him more afraid.

Then, he heard whimpering at the last crash and Box began scratching at the door. Box had always been a great judge of character and T wondered if he should venture into the garage once again.

"Are you sure, boy?" T asked Box who was still scratching at the door and barking at T for his assistance.

For Angelin

"For Angelin," he hailed softly, unlocking the door and turning the knob. As light once more illuminated the messy room made by the crate monster, Box rushed in while T remained on guard. He saw Box behind some fallen boxes near the end of the shelving, licking something... or someone.

"Who is it?" T asked as Box responded with a whine. Then he saw the dark outline of what looked like a hand patting Box's head. Box then flipped onto his back inviting whoever it was to rub his tummy.

"Who's there? Show yourself!" T demanded and he saw the crate rising again. From behind the shelving, the being revealed itself – a green-patched, yellow-skinned, slim-bodied creature with an actual crate for its head! T was too scared to move or even react.

Then, he fainted.

Chapter 4

T woke up on the dismantled fort with Box licking his face. Thinking what happened must have been a dream, he told Box of what he dreamt and was glad to know it wasn't real.

"I think it must have been an alien. Imagine if that really happened," he told Box gazing at the ceiling.

"Really happened," repeated a voice coming from behind his head, startling T as he scrambled frantically to his feet.

"What-what- who are you?!" asked T out of breath, the sight of the crate-headed alien filling him with fear again.

"I am me," replied the alien.

"You don't have a name?" T asked.

"What is a name? Is it something one finds?" it asked back.

"No, it's something given to you when you're born," T explained, not letting his guard down.

"Given by whom?" the alien asked again.

"By parents."

"What are parents?"

"They're the people who make you."

"Oh. I don't remember being made. I just appeared so maybe I have no parents," said the alien.

"Well, you need a name," T said, getting friendly with the alien as she grew on him. He studied her trying to come up with a name, and his eyes stopped on the writing on the crate.

"How about Wrecks? Seems like a great name for you, especially after what you did to the garage," he told her.

"I have a name. Thank you, Earthling," Wrecks said.

"My name's T," he said, "and my friend here is Box." Box barked in glee.

"Friend. May I have one?" Wrecks asked.

"You can have two only if you come in peace!"

Chapter 5

"Why are you wearing the crate on your head?" T asked Wrecks. "Are you afraid to show your face?"

"No, T. When I tripped and fell against the metallic structure, I bumped my head and it swelled in size just as the crate fell onto me and became stuck," Wrecks explained.

"How long would it take to go down to its normal size?" T asked her, appalled by her situation.

"In two of your Earth days," Wrecks responded.

"Hey, that's when my birthday is."

"Birthday?" Wrecks asked puzzled.

"It's the day when you're born. I'll be ten years old and I'm not looking forward to growing up," said T, explaining to Wrecks his issue.

"What is growing up?"

"That's when you have to stop being you and become another version of you that's not fun, which really isn't you."

"Then why grow up?"

"Because that's what people are supposed to do. But I have two days left so let's make the best of it. Box?"

And Box sprang to his feet off the floor and barked.

"Let's go to Angelin!"

"Is this something grown-downs do?" Wrecks asked again.

"You've never used your imagination?!"

Fact of Life #3: Imagination can take you on epic adventures

"Welcome to Angelin! Home of the Angelinites and the Great Warrior Bird!" T introduced to Wrecks. They were standing on top of a hill, overlooking the greenest of hills that were littered with towering, beautiful trees.

"Isn't it amazing?" T asked rhetorically, wearing his red-and-blue armour given to him by the Angelinites for his ongoing protection of their village.

"It reminds me of the awe-inspiring stellar systems I've come across," Wrecks responded none the wiser, as she too wore armour and a huge helmet on the crate.

The trio were marching along a path which led to the Angelinite village when they heard shrieking coming from the distance.

"Oh no! The Angelinites! Quick! We must save them!" T ordered the company, leading the charge as they all gave haste.

"What's attacking the Angelinites?" Wrecks asked.

"Kringers! They're foul, flying, hair-stealing critters! They cut the hair off anyone and carry it back to their nest to devour!" T explained, drawing his sword out as they neared the village. They were greeted by the wailing villagers and the black-shelled, flying Kringers. The Kringers were as big as Wrecks' crate and the Angelinites were a tall, brown-skinned people with lovely green hair.

"You won't be having hair here today!" T shouted at the Kringers, gaining their attention. The Kringers swarmed together and flew towards the adventurers. T began swinging his mighty sword, Box howled and turned into a humanoid version of himself, and Wrecks swung her nun-chucks so fast, it blew the Kringers away.

"You're good at this," T told her, continuing to swing his sword and knocking the Kringers out. Seeing that their flying comrades had fallen, the rest of the Kringers quit chasing the Angelinites and focused their attacks on the trio. Now, the Kringers were ten-fold in number as they overwhelmed T, Box and Wrecks, and when all hope seemed to vanish – a loud, battle-cried "caw" roared through the village.

"Yes! The Great Warrior Bird!" screamed T with delight as the large, brown-headed and yellow-crested bird flew down closely over them, scaring the Kringers. As soon as the trio got free, they continued their defence of the village with the aid of the Great Warrior Bird.

"We owe great thanks to you, Great Warrior Bird," praised the Angelinite leader, "and as well as you three – Sir T and Sir Box and Lady Wrecks."

"It's our duty!" T said, banging his sword against the metal plate of his armour.

"We're happy to do it again," Wrecks offered as she swung her nun-chucks. As Box reverted back to his dog form, he realised there was a Kringer claw gripping onto his tail and spun in circles giving chase to it in a humorous manner. It was the first time Wrecks was heard laughing as T gleefully joined in.

Fact of Life #4: Laughs are better shared with a friend

Chapter 6

"Were Box and you born to the same parents?" Wrecks asked T, walking through the living room back at T's home, looking at the pictures on the walls and shelf. She made sure the crate didn't bump into anything.

"No way! Box is a dog so he has dog parents, and I have human parents! Even though we're not from the same species and bloodline, it doesn't change the fact that we're best of friends and family," T told her with pride. He was afraid to ask more about her origins as she said she didn't remember having parents.

"You can be both family and friends?" Wrecks asked, trying to make sense of the idea.

"Sure you can. You can even be our family because love is universal. At least, that's what I like to believe," T said to her.

"But you've only known me today," Wrecks said with good reason, "I could be the doom of this galaxy or a galactic fugitive on the run from Pyrilion bounty hunters!"

"Well, so far you've posed no threat to us, and you even brought me here when I fainted in the garage," T stated.

Box arf'd, wagging his tail.

"When I first met Box," T began, "he was just a puppy – alone and abandoned near a dumpster. I was seven when I saw him, picked him up and brought him home. I fed him and bathed him, and I've never met a more grateful being. I named him Box because he'd always stay in the box-turned-bed I made for him till he grew too big. All that puppy at the dumpster needed was love, and we've been friends and family since."

And Wrecks understood.

Fact of Life #5: Helping others is good for the soul

Chapter 7

The next day came like any other, and T hurried downstairs to find his sister and Box in the kitchen as he decided to eat cereal. He kept looking in the direction of the garage, hoping his sister would soon leave home to go to the mall that Saturday morning. She left him to go upstairs, and T and Box rushed into the garage carrying a refilled bowl of cereal and milk.

"Wrecks? Are you here still?" he asked, hoping she did not leave just yet.

"Behind the metallic structure," she said, raising her crated head from the floor.

"I brought you some cereal," T said offering her the bowl of cereal.

"Thank you," she said holding the bowl. "What do I do with it?"

"You eat it. Aren't you hungry?" he asked her.

"Oh. I'm not hungry, but I have a crate on my head so I can't eat anyway," she said.

A noise came from the room next door and T panicked.

"Be quiet. I'll be back!" he instructed Wrecks as he left the garage, locking the door.

"What were you doing in there?" T's sister asked him, fully dressed for the mall. T's mind raced frantically to come up with a valid excuse.

"Box needed to get his screwdriver!" was the first thing that blurted from his mouth. Even Box knew how stupid T sounded as he face-pawed himself.

"Okay then," his sister replied to his loony answer, "just stay out of trouble. I'm leaving now to go to the mall. You better not burn the house down by the time I get back. Love you."

She kissed him on his head.

And he wiped the yucky gesture off.

Chapter 8

"Is your head ever going to go down?" T asked
Wrecks impatiently. She lay upside down on the couch

with the crate on the carpet as they watched TV. He wanted to see what she looked like without the crate.

"It will, soon enough," Wrecks answered.

"You aliens are so..." T said drifting into thought and he remembered something. Maybe it was because there was an actual alien in his living room whom he was watching cartoons with, and she implied she came in peace. But she did imply something else.

"Are you really a galactic fugitive on the run from alien bounty hunters?" he asked her. She turned her gaze from the TV to T, and paused for a moment.

"No, I'm not," Wrecks answered.

"So what's your mission? Why did you come to Earth?" T asked.

"I heard your voice from across the galaxy," she said, surprising T.

"My voice? How is that possible?!" he asked bewildered.

"If you look up and talk to the stars, they do hear you," Wrecks explained, "and I heard your voice so I steered my ship to your direction."

"You came to Earth... for me?"

"Indeed, I did."

T felt special. The first recorded alien life-form he knew about came to him – the avid stargazer!

"Are you supposed to take me back with you? 'Cause that would be the coolest thing ever!" T exclaimed.

"No, I think I'm here to help you with your problem," Wrecks explained.

"Growing up?"

"Yes."

"Oh," T sighed as he was reminded his birthday was tomorrow. The big 1-0. Box sensed T's mood change and sat at his feet to let T know he was there for him.

"How old are you, Wrecks?" he asked her, wondering if she went through what he was going through. But she's not a human, he thought.

"I'm not sure. I'm about four and a half stellar trips old which may equal to nine Earth years," Wrecks said. T was surprised – he was older than the alien! But she was a space explorer and having no family, she was already grown up and probably never had the chance of growing up. In that moment, he forgot about his problem and felt sorry for her.

"Follow me, Wrecks. I want to show you something," T said leading her and Box to the backyard. The backyard was bigger than the front yard, and the grass was a healthy green and short. There were a couple fruit trees and one towering non-fruit tree with a bench located beneath it.

"This is probably my most favourite place on Earth," T told Wrecks as the trio sat the same way they did inside.

"Why is that?" Wrecks asked, wiggling her feet as the breeze blew.

"It's the feeling I get when I sit out here. Like this is what the world is supposed to be 'cause there isn't any nature indoors. And I sit alone on this bench. I see the wind blow by and I hear the songs of the trees, and I sit here alone because no one else comes."

"I'm here now, and so is Box," said the sympathetic alien.

"And that's what makes this the best moment of my life," said T with a smile on his face.

Fact of Life #6: You don't need much to have everything

Chapter 9

After spending a long time outside, they went back inside to the kitchen and T got something to eat. Wrecks looked like she didn't mind, but T thought she must be starving by now.

"Are you sure you're not hungry?" T asked her.

"Indeed I'm sure. I can survive without solids and liquids for quite a while," Wrecks explained.

"Wow!" T exclaimed, "not being able to eat and drink for that long?! That sounds like the coolest thing ever!"

"You need to consume often during the day?" Wrecks asked him making an observation.

"Yeah, I have to. Otherwise, I'd starve! But I eat when I can since the food doesn't come so easy," T told her. "I wish I could be like you, so I can survive for days. That'd be perfect!"

"Perfect? What's perfect?" Wrecks questioned.

"It's like being able to become flawless in every way. For instance, if I have unlimited energy I won't need to eat or drink ever again. And I won't ever get tired!" T explained.

"Won't you miss your dreams?"

"What do you mean?"

"If you won't ever get tired again, you won't be able to sleep. Not being able to sleep would deny you of having dreams," Wrecks said. T hadn't thought it through. He loved the dreams he had because sometimes he'd do amazing things in them. His dreams were just like his imagination, only he didn't know he was asleep so the dreams felt real to him.

"You're right. I'd be so bored especially when Box is asleep. You know something, with a crate stuck on your head, I sometimes forget that you're more intelligent than you look!"

Fact of Life #7: Being perfect is boring

Chapter 10

Night approached and T was able to hide Wrecks in his room, hoping that they'd stay awake till his birthday came. He was more excited to see what Wrecks looked like when her head was back to normal size. T's sister had arrived back home earlier, and now she was wishing T a good night as she went to bed. T wondered if she went to the mall to get him something for his birthday, and then he remembered his growing up issue. Wasn't Wrecks supposed to help him with that?

"Hey Wrecks," T whispered as he did not want to let his sister hear him at the risk of getting caught, "I really don't want to grow up."

"Why do you have to, T? Don't you have a choice?" Wrecks asked him.

"I don't think I do. My sister grew up when she was ten because of my parents, and it's the same way for me. I don't want to be a disappointment, but I know if I grow up I would be disappointing myself," T said with sadness in his voice.

"Maybe I will say something to make you feel better," Wrecks said.

"Something like what?" T asked.

"I don't know, I haven't thought of it yet," she replied as it fell short of T's expectation.

The radio clock in his room crept closer to midnight as T tried his best to stay awake lying in bed, with Wrecks in the same sitting position with her feet on the mattress.

"I can feel my head shrinking," she finally said.

"Really?!" T said as he shot up from his pillow in excitement. "It's too bad Box isn't in here."

Wrecks stood on her feet as the crate started shifting on her head as it shrank, T's eyes opening wide awaiting the big reveal. He saw her eyes disappear from the holes as the crate lowered onto her body. As it touched the ground, everything got silent. T scrambled out of bed and approached the crate cautiously. He wished Box was there because as much as he was excited, he was half frightened. Then, the crate lifted off the ground and the alien revealed herself. Her head was yellow like her body, was shaped like a wide upside-down pencil and she had four eyes.

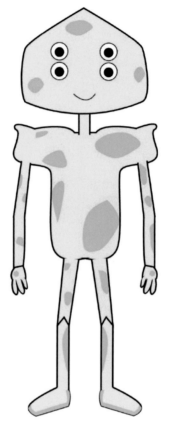

"So that's what you look like!" T exclaimed as he clamped his mouth shut hoping he didn't wake his sister. He went to the window and whispered loudly at Box to wake up, but he didn't respond. He quickly made a paper airplane and flew it successfully into Box, who awoke startled. He looked up at T and presented Wrecks to him, giving an 'arf!'.

"Happy birthday, T," she said, surprising T as he forgot about the time. It was a few minutes after midnight.

"Oh dear…" T said, sighing. "Can this night not end? That way in the morning, I won't be something I'm not."

"But it's okay, T," Wrecks told him. "Whether you're ten or one hundred and ten, you'll still be you. Always be you and you won't regret it one bit."

"How would that help if I'm grown up?" T asked her.

"Who creates the cartoons we watched on TV?" she asked him back.

"Cartoons? People, I guess," he responded, confused by Wrecks' question.

"Are the people adults?" she asked, following up with another question.

"Yes, they are," he said still confused.

"And yet they're making cartoons. Perhaps, those adults are not grown up just yet but are still growing up. Maybe they won't even be fully grown up when they get old. Therefore, you don't need to grow up right now." She explained her point as it made sense to T. He felt an enormous weight lifted off his chest as he came to realise:

Fact of Life #8: Adults make cartoons so why grow up?

Chapter 11

It was half past five in the morning, as the creaking of the bedroom door woke T from his slumber. He rubbed his eyes and looked around the room, noticing Wrecks had just left. He raced out of bed, down the stairs and found Wrecks walking towards the door to the garage, with the crate in her hands.

"Wrecks? Where are you going?" he asked her.

"I have to go now, T. My mission here is complete and I'm no longer needed here," Wrecks explained.

"That's not true! We're family! I need you!" he told her as sadness came over him.

"I'm sorry, T, but I must continue on my own mission. I won't forget you or the things you've taught me and shown me," Wrecks said with appreciation.

"I won't forget you either, Wrecks," he cried as he dashed to hug her tightly. The alien welcomed the embrace as all four of her eyes closed, hugging him back.

Fact of Life #9: Saying goodbye always suck

"There's one more thing I have to show you, Wrecks. Stay here," T told her. He raced to the front door to get Box inside, and they both rushed to the kitchen. Wrecks was ordered to join them as she saw T preparing breakfast: both toast and cereal. Certainly, T wasn't going to combine the two meals again! But instead he prepared both for the three of them.

"You must be hungry NOW," he told her and she realised she was. "Have a taste, Wrecks."

She took a bite off the buttered toast, chewed and swallowed. Then, she took a spoonful of the cereal and milk, chewed and swallowed. T had the widest grin and Box barked with glee as they both saw the most satisfied look on Wrecks' face as she learned one last thing from her human friend:

Fact of Life #10: Toast and Cereal are the best things in the Universe!

End

Message from the Author

I'd like to thank you, the reader, for exploring my imagination with me. You've escaped your reality into another universe with the swipe of the pages and the words existing on them. Whether you're 9 years old or 90, never stop being who you are.

After all, being yourself is who you will always be.

- Steffan

Made in the USA
Middletown, DE
20 April 2017